_____
Your name

1

Illustrated by **Tony Vecchio**
Copyright © 1993 James B. Boulden   Printed in USA
Boulden Publishing, P.O. Box 1186, Weaverville, CA 96093-1186
Phone (800)238-8433, FAX (916)623-5525, E-mail jboulden@snowcrest.net

Please draw a picture of yourself.

How do you feel about your hair? _____

_____

_____

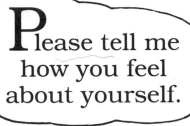

Please tell me how you feel about yourself.

Sometimes I feel different because I am

_____

_____

What bothers me the most about myself is

_____

_____

The reason it bothers me is _____

_____

_____

One good thing about being this way is

_____

_____

I used to think mean things about myself.

What is a mean thing you say to yourself?

I am _____

I felt that other kids were better than me.

Please complete these sentences.

I am a _____ kid.

Losing makes me feel _____

_____

When other kids win, I feel _____

_____

It feels _____

_____ to be alone with myself.

Other kids are _____

than I am because I _____

_____

Sometimes I would think "poor me."
Feeling sorry for myself made things worse.

Do you sometimes feel sorry for yourself?

_____

Does it make you feel better or worse?

_____

I started to grow tall in the third grade.
Soon I could run faster than ever before.
It felt good to be able to do something well.

What is something you are good at? _____

_____

When I started to like myself,
other kids seemed to like me better too.

What do your friends like best about you?

_____

_____

One day my teacher said that I was special.
She said there had never ever
been anyone just like me.

In what way do you feel special? _____
_____
_____

Everyone is important in some special way. Jordan, my cat, makes me feel important when he licks my face.

What is something that makes you feel

important? _____

_____

Games are fun.
Draw a picture of you playing with a classmate.

Some kids tease me because I laugh a lot.
That is okay.
I don't have to make everyone like me.

It helps me to laugh when I am feeling bad. There is always something funny to think about.

Draw a face showing how you feel when you laugh.

Sometimes I think everything is my fault. Most of the time, this is not true at all.

What is something you felt bad about that was not your fault? _____

_____

_____

Other times, I blame all my problems on other people.

*In what ways are you responsible for your own behavior?*_____

_____

_____

I listen to mean things others say about me. Often I don't hear the nice things.

What is something good someone said about you? _____

_____

Sometimes I forget the good things I have done and remember the bad things.

What is something you have done that you are proud of? _____

_____

I stay away from kids that try to make me feel bad.

Why do some kids make fun of other kids?

_____

_____

This year I learned to ride my bike to school. It feels good to take care of myself.

What are three things you do to take care of yourself?

1) _____

2) _____

3) _____

23

I feel good when I do what I say I will do. This year I am doing my homework on time.

What is something you have done that

you said you would do? _____

_____

I used to try to be perfect, but that never worked. Everyone makes mistakes.

Write about a mistake that you have made.

_____

_____

I learn something every time I make a mistake.

What is something you learned from your mistake? _____

_____

I feel good about myself when I help other people.

What is a nice thing you have done for

someone? _____

_____

How do you think they felt? _____

_____

*P*lease complete these sentences.

I feel happy at home when I _____

_____

_____

I feel good at school when I _____

_____

I have fun with friends when I _____

_____

_____

I do well in school when I _____

_____

My body feels better when I _____

_____

_____

What three wishes would you like to make about your life?

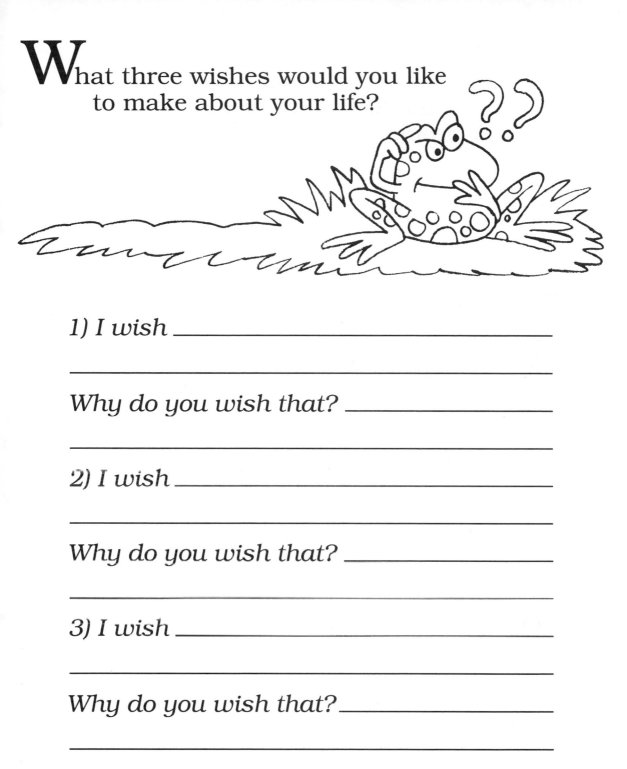

1) I wish _____

_____

Why do you wish that? _____

_____

2) I wish _____

_____

Why do you wish that? _____

_____

3) I wish _____

_____

Why do you wish that? _____

_____

It is hard for me to change how I think and feel about myself.
Other people can help me if I let them.

Who do you feel you can talk to? _____

_____

What would you like to talk about? _____

_____

RESOURCES FOR CHILDREN IN DISTRESS

Used by 15,000 Institutions   **700,000 books in Print**

ACTIVITY BOOKS

Age appropriate selected materials are available from kindergarten to Sr. High School. The books feature ethnic diversity and are gender specific when necessary.

Bereavement ✪ *Divorce* ✪ *Remarriage* ✪ *Single Parent*
Blended Family ✪ *Self-esteem* ✪ *Physical Abuse* ✪ *Sexual Abuse*
Parental Substance Abuse ✪ *Feelings* ✪ *Bully/Victim*
AIDS Awareness ✪ *Serious Illness* ✪ *Anger Control*
Conflict Resolution

REPRODUCIBLE WORKBOOKS

Consumable companions to the activity books, each workbook contains key graphics and exercises from the corresponding activity books. Now each child can have their own counseling materials to mark up and take home to discuss with their parents. The cost to the institution for reproducing these materials is minimal.

SUPPORTIVE MATERIALS

Feelings posters and draw-a-face packs assist children in identifying their feelings. Art completion exercises plus puzzles and games bring laughter and excitement to the discussion of emotional issues. Guidelines are available for parents in providing positive support for their children.

PHONE FOR FREE CATALOG (800) 238-8433